For the other messy Jess
~ P. B.

tiger tales
5 River Road, Suite 128, Wilton, CT 06897
Published in the United States 2015
Text and illustrations copyright © 2015 Paula Bowles
ISBN-13: 978-1-58925-133-5
ISBN-10: 1-58925-133-4
Printed in China
LTP/1400/0991/0914
10 9 8 7 6 5 4 3 2 1

For more insight and activities,
visit us at www.tigertalesbooks.com

Messy Jesse

by

Paula Bowles

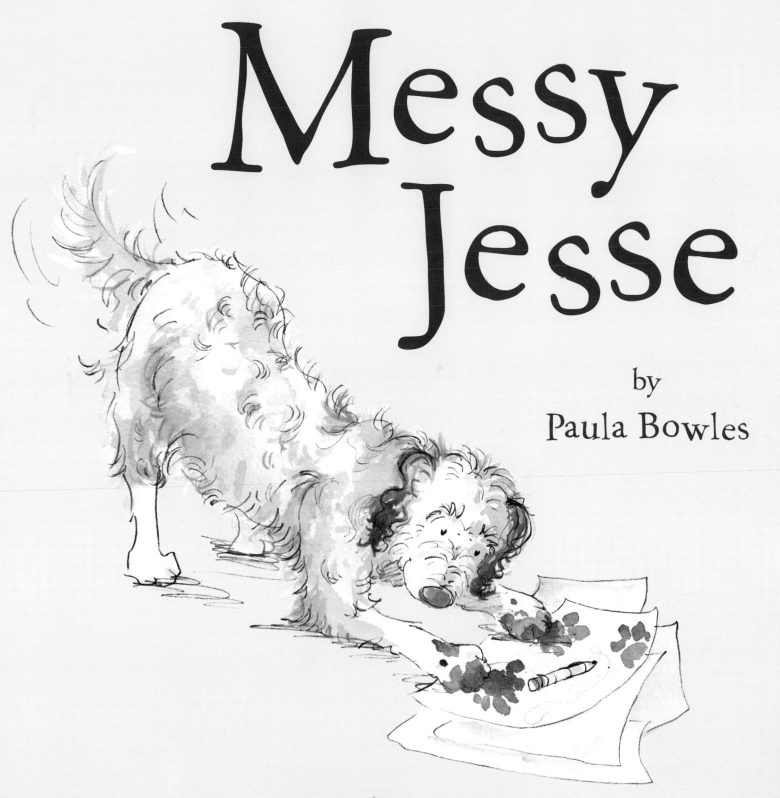

tiger tales

This is
Messy Jesse.

He loved having fun
and he was really good at
making things!

Paper hats,
delicious cakes,

and blanket forts!

But he was **especially** good at making . . .

And the more
Jesse played,

the more **mess** he made!

And so the mess grew . . .

and grew . . .

and grew!

Until one day . . .

. . . all his favorite toys
had disappeared!

He couldn't find his crunchy **bone**.
He couldn't even find his
cozy **blanket!**

But worst of all . . .

. . . the other pets couldn't find Jesse!

He had disappeared, too!

Rabbit hopped into the
mess to find Jesse.
But then
Rabbit got lost!

Cat tried
next.

She climbed in very carefully,
but soon she was lost, too!

Now, only Hamster
was left.

He dove in to
find the others . . .

I'm over here!

And then,
at last,
Messy Jesse
had an **idea**.

He started to put away all the paper and
pens, the pots and pans,
and the paint and brushes.
Ever so slowly, things reappeared.

First, Jesse found Cat.

Then he found Rabbit
and Hamster.

He found his **blanket** beneath a pile of hats,

his **bone** in a shoe,

and his **favorite toys** under his blanket.

Until finally, he looked around and saw that everything was . . .

very, very clean.

"Hooray!"

everyone cheered.

Now there was space . . .
to make
a mess **all**
over again!